Ginger the Clumsy Dog

by
Patty Steponovich

Ginger the Clumsy Dog
by Patty Steponovich
Illustrated by Pearly Lim

Published by
Euclid House Publishing
Long Beach, California

Library of Congress Control Number: 2021918633
ISBN: 978-1-7379151-0-2 (paperback)
        978-1-7379151-1-9 (Kindle)

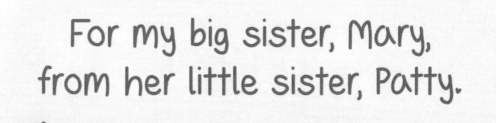

For my big sister, Mary,
from her little sister, Patty.

Mary lived in a pretty house with a hill in the backyard.

But sometimes she felt lonely. Mary's friends said she should get a pet to keep her company.

"Maybe someday," she would say.

One night Mary was at the store picking up
a roast for dinner.

In the parking lot, she spotted a little,
brown-eyed dog perched in a shopping cart.

Mary decided to take him home.

"If I can't find your owner,
I'm going to call you Joey,"
she said as they rode to her house
with the hill in the backyard.

Mary spent the next week trying to find Joey's owner.
She put up signs and called the local animal shelter,
but no one seemed to be looking for him.

A few weeks later, as Mary was leaving the shopping mall, she saw a dog wandering around by himself.

His fur stuck out like the quills of a porcupine, and he didn't have a collar or a chip.

"Joey would love to have a friend like you,"

Mary said as she lifted the dog into her car.

"I'll call you Zeke."

Once again, she tried to find the owner, and once again, no one seemed to be looking for this little dog.

Now that she had two little dogs,
Mary never felt lonely anymore.

Joey and Zeke got along well
and loved to play together on
the hill in her backyard.

Then one day, Mary went to the store to buy some fabric for a new quilt. Outside the store was a box with a little curly-haired puppy inside.

The doggie was cute and friendly, but looked sad. "If I can't find your owner, I'm going to call you Ginger," said Mary as she picked up the box with the puppy in it and took it home.

That night, she smiled
as Ginger played with Joey
and Zeke on the hill in her backyard.

Joey, Zeke, and Ginger become best friends.

They had breakfast together.

They jumped on the furniture together.

They snuggled on Mary's lap together.

And they climbed and played on the hill in the backyard together.

Both Joey and Zeke were experienced hill climbers, but Ginger was still a little puppy. She had some trouble with the hill in the backyard.

One afternoon, Joey and Zeke and Ginger were high on the hill when Ginger rolled down the hill like a tumbleweed and landed with a thud.

Mary heard Ginger yelp.
She was hurt.

Ginger couldn't stand
on one of her legs, so Mary picked
her up and took her to the vet.

"You'll be okay, little girl," said Mary.
But everybody was scared,
especially Joey and Zeke.

After the vet took some x-rays of Ginger's leg, she said, "This pup has a broken leg." She put a little cast on Ginger's little leg.

Ginger could still walk, but now she could only use three legs. She couldn't go on the hill in the backyard with Joey and Zeke until she got better.

With the little cast on her little leg,
Ginger was extra clumsy.

One day, she fell off Mary's bed and
landed on the floor with a clunk.

And the next day,
Ginger ran into a sliding door!

While Ginger had her cast on, Joey and Zeke spent more time inside to keep her company.

But sometimes they still liked to play on the hill in the backyard. Ginger could only watch.

"You'll be back out there with them soon," Mary said.

Sure enough, after a few weeks
Ginger's leg had healed.

Mary took her to the vet,
and she removed the cast.

Soon,
Ginger was back
to normal.

And finally . . .

They had breakfast together.

They jumped on the furniture together.

They snuggled on
Mary's lap together.

And they climbed
and played on the hill in
the backyard together.

And Mary was never lonely again.

The End.

About the Author

Patty Steponovich has been an Art teacher
for over 30 years in Long Beach, California.
She has 3 children and 4 rescue cats
but loves dogs as well!
This book is inspired by her sister Mary
and three true life dogs, Joey, Zeke,
and of course, Ginger.

Joey

Zeke

Ginger

Made in the USA
Monee, IL
03 October 2021

79285779R00021